Socks

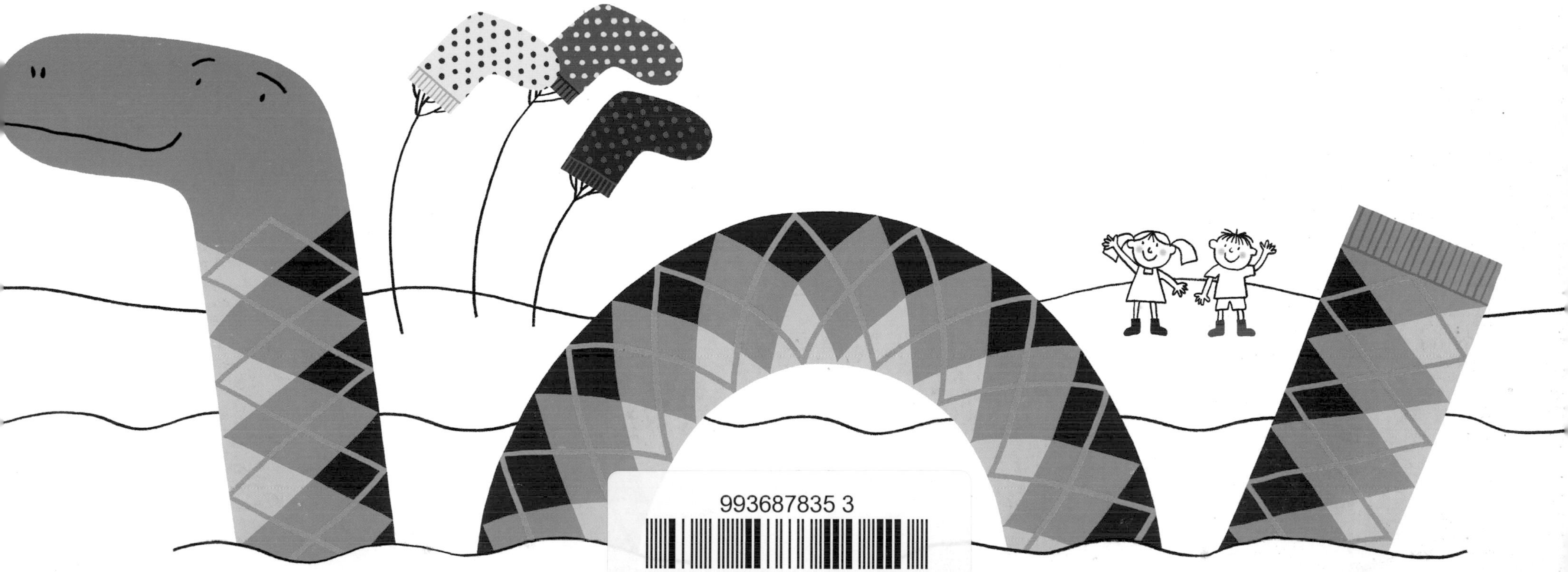

For Jon,
who wears the finest **socks**
N. S.

For the **sockalicious** Arthur, Florence and Cecily,
with my love
E. L.

The refrain in this book was inspired by the wonderfully named
Choccywoccydoodah, a chocolaterie in Brighton

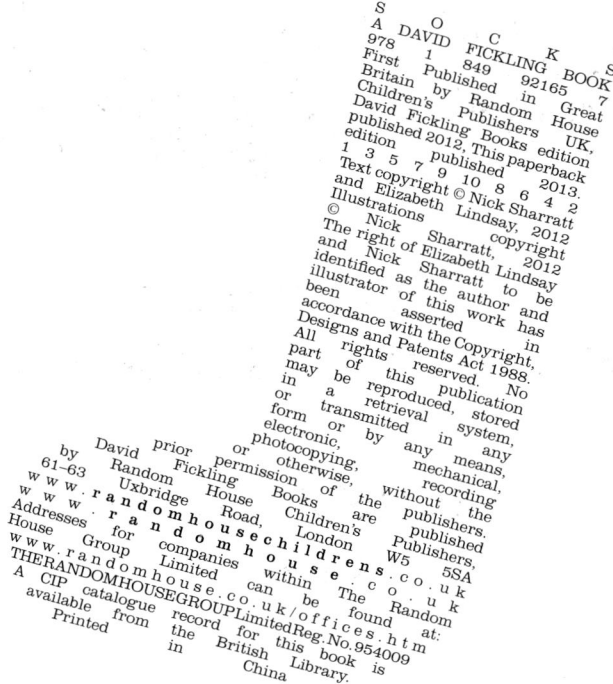

SOCKS
A DAVID FICKLING BOOK
978 1 849 92165 7
First Published in Great Britain by Random House Children's Publishers UK, David Fickling Books edition published 2012, This paperback edition published 2013.
1 3 5 7 9 10 8 6 4 2
Text copyright © Nick Sharratt and Elizabeth Lindsay, 2012
Illustrations copyright © Nick Sharratt, 2012
The right of Elizabeth Lindsay and Nick Sharratt to be identified as the author and illustrator of this work has been asserted in accordance with the Copyright, Designs and Patents Act 1988.
David Fickling Books are published by Random House Children's Publishers UK, 61–63 Uxbridge Road, London W5 5SA
www.randomhousechildrens.co.uk
www.randomhouse.co.uk
Addresses for companies within The Random House Group Limited can be found at: www.randomhouse.co.uk/offices.htm
THE RANDOM HOUSE GROUP Limited Reg. No. 954009
A CIP catalogue record for this book is available from the British Library.
Printed in China

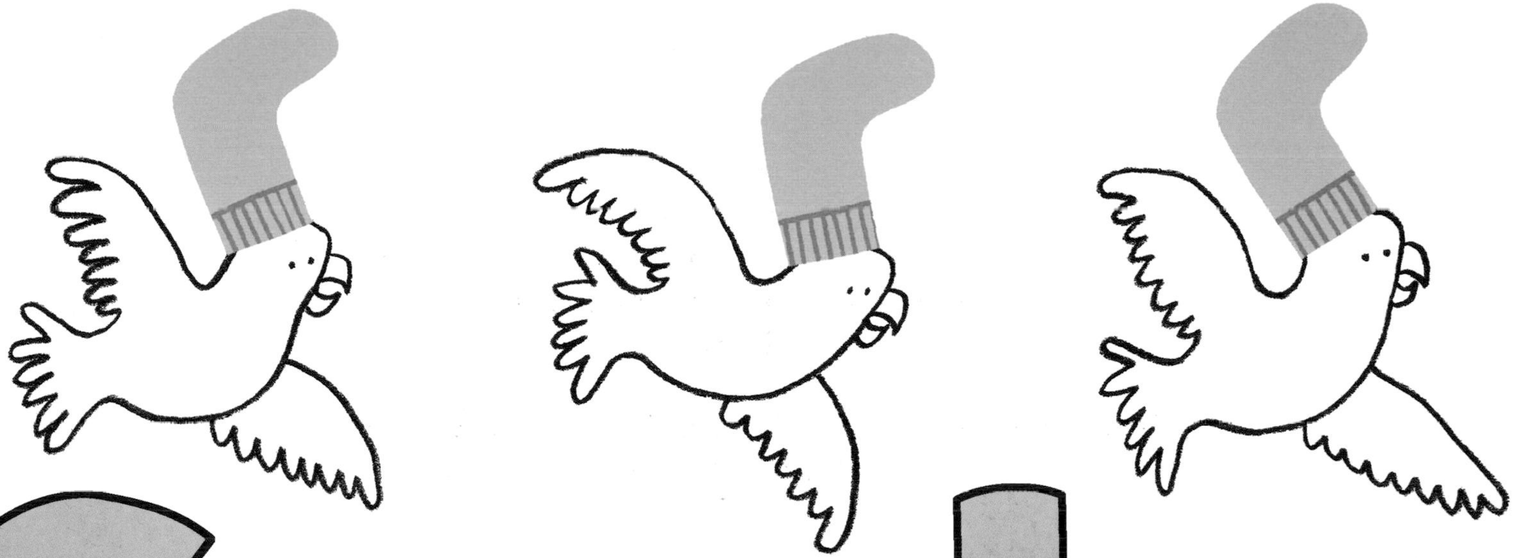

Socks

Written by
Nick Sharratt & Elizabeth Lindsay

Illustrated by
Nick Sharratt

David Fickling Books

SOCKYWOCKYDOODAH!

A-tick-a-tick-a-tock

What's the time in **Sockland?**

It's always **SOCKS O'CLOCK!**

SOCKYWOCKYDOODAH!

The **sockerel** struts his stuff

And **sock-a-bloomin'-doodles**

Till the hens cry, **"THAT'S ENOUGH!"**

Put a sock in it!

Nice horsies

SOCKYWOCKYDOODAH!

The happy cows go **MOO**

Sockish ponies, aren't they sweet?

And teeny tiny too.

SOCKYWOCKYDOODAH!

So what do we have here?

A greedy-guts called **Goldisocks**

And three cross bears, **OH DEAR!**

SOCKYWOCKY-CHOOCHOO-TRAIN!

For **Socktown** take a seat
There everybody's wearing **socks**
And not just on their **FEET**!

SOCKYWOCKYDOODAH!
Popsock-a-lula-bop!
That **socksophone** just makes you feel
Like **JIVING** till you drop!

Sock 'n' Roll!

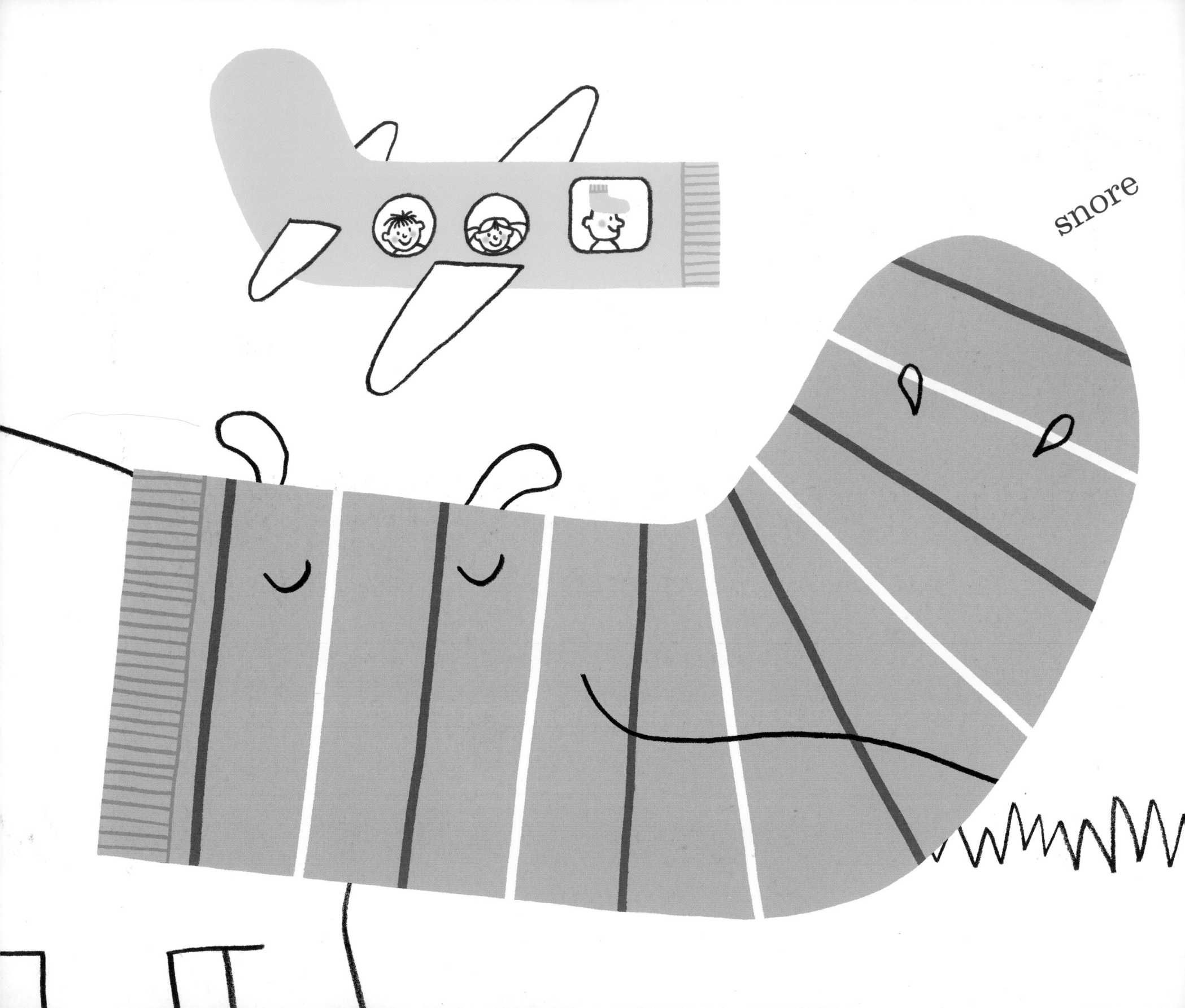

snore

SOCKYWOCK-ADVENTURE!

From our **sock plane** we can spy

A dozing **hipposockamus**

As **sockatoos** fly by.

SOCKYWOCKY-SNAP-SNAP!

Beware the **sockodile**
Especially when she flashes you
Her **socking** GREAT BIG SMILE!

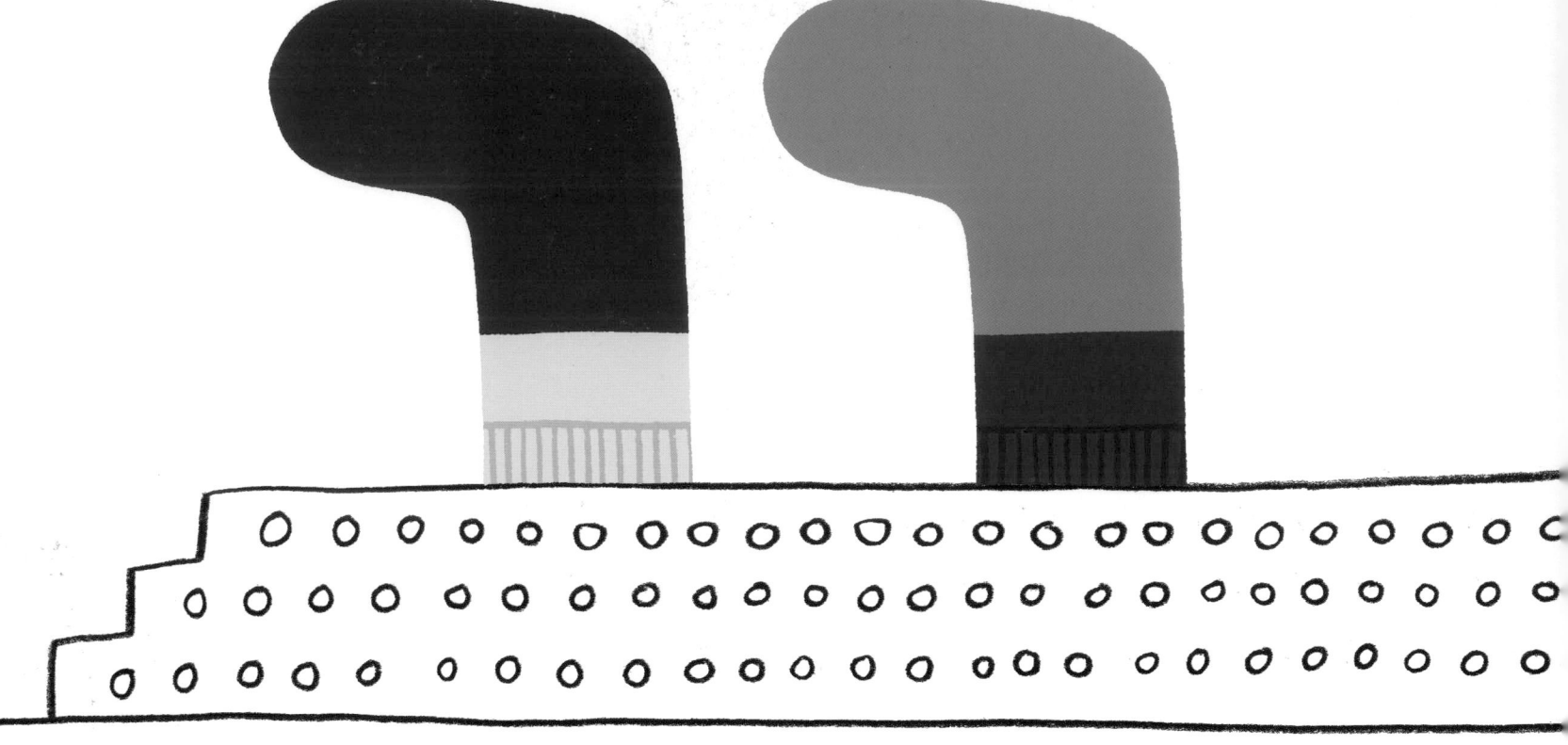

SOCKYWOCKY-ALL-ABOARD!

Let's cruise the **socky seas**

What lies beneath the salty waves?

We'd like an **ANSWER** please!

mmm, tasty!

SOCKYWOCKYDOODAH!
By our little **sockmarine**

There's a **socktopus**, a **mersock**

And a **sockshark** looking **MEAN!**

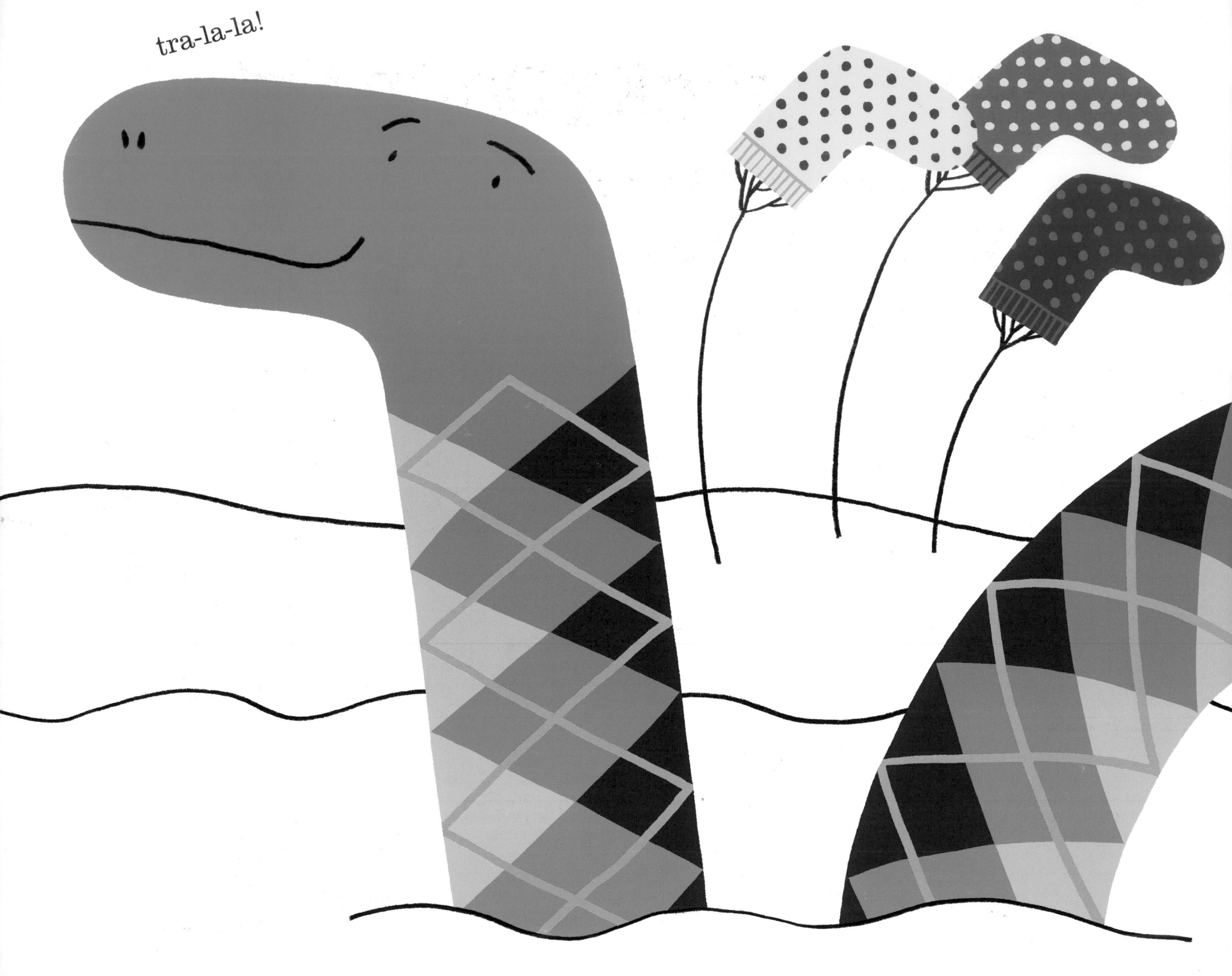

SOCKYWOCKYDOODAH!

As **sock trees** gently sway

Wave to the **Sock Ness Monster**

On her summer holiday!

SOCKYWOCKY-SLEEPY-YAWN!

It's **bedsocks** time, OK?

We've had the most

SOCKTASTIC,

sockalicious,

SOCK-ELASTIC,

socks-amazing,

SOCKS-A-CRAZY,

sock-a-zooming,

SOCK-A-WAVY,

Sock-it-to-me-round-the-clocky

SOCKYWOCKYDOODAH-DAY!

(phew!)

More books illustrated by Nick Sharratt:

JUST IMAGINE

Nick Sharratt   Pippa Goodhart

Let your imagination run wild – what will YOU CHOOSE to be?

YOU CHOOSE

Nick Sharratt   Pippa Goodhart

Giles Andreae   Nick Sharratt
Pants

Giles Andreae   Nick Sharratt
more Pants

A fin-tastic sequel to Shark in the Park!
SHARK in the Dark!
GLOWS in the DARK!
Nick Sharratt

Shark in the Dark!